The Mouse Family's New Home

BY Edith Kunhardt

ILLUSTRATED BY Diane Dawson

Golden Press • New York
Western Publishing Company, Inc., Racine, Wisconsin

Mr. and Mrs. Mouse and their children, Maureen and Malcolm, were just moving into their new home under the floorboards of a big old house. They put down their suitcases with a sigh of relief.

"No dawdling, now. We must find food and furniture before night falls," said Mrs. Mouse.

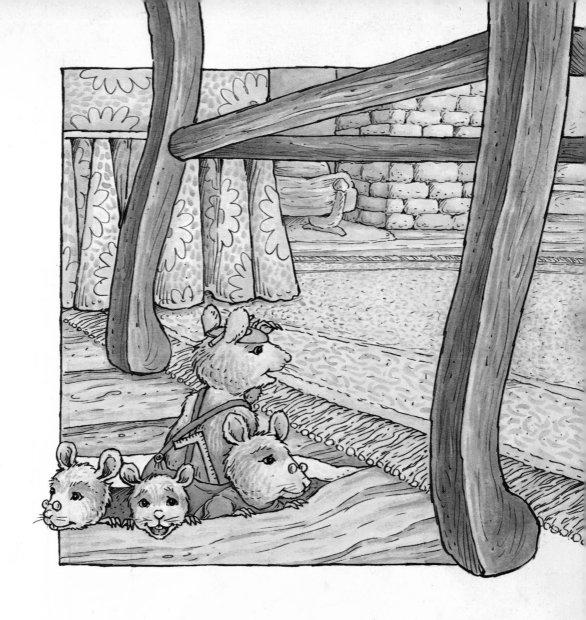

So they crept to their new door and peered out.
Everything was quiet. No one was about.

"Look!" Mr. Mouse exclaimed, pointing.
Everyone followed him to a large lollipop that
was lying under the sofa. "This will make a magnificent
dining room table. Help me carry it home,"
Mr. Mouse said.

When the lollipop was safely inside, each mouse
scurried off in a different direction.

In the kitchen, Mr. Mouse found some sticks.

"Hmm," he said to himself. "These will be perfect
for table legs."

He dragged the sticks home
and set about building the table.

Meanwhile Mrs. Mouse had climbed into an open bureau drawer.

"My stars! Just what I need for a sofa," she exclaimed, pummeling a soft fragrant pillow right out of the drawer and plop! onto the floor.

In the pantry Maureen found some funny soft
red and black strips.

"I shall braid these into a rug for our new home,"
cried Maureen triumphantly.

Malcolm was in the bathroom, peering at a cake of soap.

"This will make a great bathtub," he thought.

He pushed the soap off the sink, scampered down the drainpipe, and began to slide the soap across the floor.

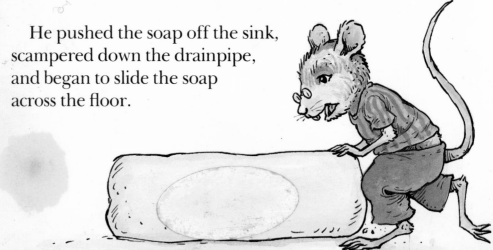

"Malcolm! Oh, Malcolm. Please help me get these teabags back home. They'll make lovely pillows," Mrs. Mouse called as Malcolm passed the kitchen.

So they put the teabags on top of the soap and pushed them home. Then they set to work to decorate with all of their new-found treasures.

A little later, Mr. Mouse arrived with half a walnut shell. He was delighted to see all of the furniture in place.

"Here is a bowl for us, my dear," he was just saying, but he changed to, "My! How very nice everything looks!"

Suddenly they heard a voice singing, "Cheese, cheese, beautiful cheese," and Maureen entered, pushing a large piece of cheese.

"Hooray!" everyone cheered, rushing over to take a nibble.

Now they really felt at home.